Anna Shares

BY
Barbara Baker

PICTURES BY
Catharine O'Neill

DUTTON CHILDREN'S BOOKS · New York

For Billie
B.A.B.

For Laura Glenn
C.O.

Text copyright © 2004 by Barbara A. Baker
Illustrations copyright © 2004 by Catharine O'Neill
All rights reserved.

CIP Data is available.

Published in the United States 2004 by Dutton Children's Books,
a division of Penguin Young Readers Group
345 Hudson Street, New York, New York 10014
www.penguin.com

Designed by Irene Vandervoort

Manufactured in China   First Edition

1 3 5 7 9 10 8 6 4 2

ISBN 0-525-47111-1

This is Anna.

Anna plays with Justin.

Mommy brings a snack.

Two cookies for Anna.
Two cookies for Justin.

"Mine," says Anna.
Anna takes all the cookies.

"No," cries Justin.

Mommy says that
Anna must share.
Sharing is good.

Anna does not want
to share.

Mommy helps Anna to share.

Anna cries, "No, no, no!"

Justin has to go home.

Anna plays with Teddy Bear
and Bunny.

Anna gives one cookie to Teddy Bear.
Anna gives one cookie to Bunny.

Anna keeps one cookie.
Sharing is good.

Then Anna eats
all *three* cookies.

The End.